Who is Pepper Storm?

By Keshius Williams

Illustrated by TeMika Grooms

Who is Pepper Storm?

by Keshius Williams

Illustrated by TeMika Grooms

http://www.whoispepperstorm.webs.com/

ISBN-13: 978-1494363512

ISBN-10: 1494363518

Printed in the U.S.A.
First Printing, December 2013

The illustrations in this book were done in gouache, ink and pencil on paper.

The general text type was set in Comic Sans MS Bold.

Book designed by TeMika Grooms under My Muse Arts, LLC.
www.temikatheartist.com

Hi, my name is **Pepper Storm**!

And you may wonder about my name.

Pepper comes from my dark brown skin

And my daddy liked **Storm** instead of *Rain*.

I'm a typical kid who loves

ADVENTURE

And believes I can do anything.

I'm **FEARLESS;**

FREE SPIRITED;

and **FUN;**

And, did I mention I can sing?

I like to wear my afro puffs

'Cause my natural look is the best.

It makes me **PROUD** to wear my hair like this

But sometimes I wear it pressed.

My favorite subject in school is Science.

I ate chocolate

covered crickets
and a sprinkled worm.

We do experiments like

VOLCANO
ERUPTIONS

And the best part is that I learn.

I love to taste different foods

And help my mommy cook.

Can you believe I like sushi?

But my siblings all say,

"YUCK!"

My teacher says I'm a

STAR STUDENT

And I always do my best

I go to school ready to learn

And do well on every test.

In my spare time I like to

'Cause acting is my dream.

I know there's nothing I can't do

And I can be

Like an **Astronaut,**

a **Veterinarian,**

a **Teacher,**

Or even **Queen Of The World!**

I've also walked in a fashion show.

Hey everybody,

watch my **twirl!**

My favorite colors are

black,

pink, and

white

And I have fish as my pets.

I really want a little puppy

But daddy says,

"We're not ready for that yet."

My mom wants us to be well-rounded kids.

So, she gives us chores to do.

I sweep,

wash dishes,

and clean the table

To earn my allowance when I'm through.

I'm **CONFIDENT,**

ADVENTUROUS,

and **FULL OF LIFE**

and nothing is gonna hold me back

From being the beautiful butterfly that I am,

It's true and

THAT'S A FACT!

Now you know a little bit about
"Who is Pepper Storm?"

GREATNESS

is my destiny

Since the very first day I was born.

So enjoy the tales about my life

And how I came to be.

I am Pepper Storm

with
dark brown skin

And God created me!

Pepper Storm Wins

at Field Day

It was Monday and the most important, fun-filled day of the year would be here on Friday. Everyone was excited because Friday was *Field Day.* I finally get a chance to prove that I am the fastest girl in 3rd grade!

I was so *FAST* that whenever I would race, my friends wouldn't call me *Pepper Storm.* They would call me **QUICK SILVER**. I got that name because they said I was hard to catch.

Although I was the fastest girl in my class, there was one problem. My friend Samantha in the other class was fast too. We had never raced each other before, but on *Field Day,* everyone would get to see who was the fastest. We were both competing in the 100-yard dash. So, I knew I had to practice hard if I wanted to win the title of

FASTEST GIRL.

I practiced day and night.

I practiced while doing my homework.

I practiced coming home from school.

I practiced in dance class.

I even practiced in my sleep.

I practiced so much that all my sneakers had holes in them.

It was now Wednesday and everyone in 3rd grade was talking about who would win the 100-yard dash. That's when our friendly competition turned not so friendly. When I walked past Samantha in the cafeteria, she blurted out to me,

"They're not gonna call you *Quick Silver* anymore, they're gonna call you **LOSER!**"

All the kids started to laugh. I ran out of the cafeteria as fast as I could. I couldn't believe my friend would embarrass me like that. This made me so mad. I was determined that when *Field Day* came, I was going to leave her in my ***dust!***

It was now Friday and finally time for the 100-yard dash competition. Everyone would get to see who would win the title of *FASTEST GIRL*.

All of us lined up to get ready for the race. Wouldn't you know it; I was right next to Samantha. We looked at each other, but didn't say a word.

Coach said,

"Runners,

Take your marks!

Get set!

GO!"

I took off quicker than everybody. All I could think about was finishing first. As I got closer to the finish line, I heard my classmates chanting......

GO QUICK SILVER!

GO QUICK SILVER!

GO!

I ran even faster!

Just as the race was about to end, I noticed Samantha was right there next to me. I knew it was going to be a close finish. Then all of a sudden, Samantha fell. She tripped over her shoelaces and went tumbling to the ground. I was so close to the finish line that I didn't want to stop. She had said mean things to me so why should I give up the race to go and help her? I thought to myself,

Do I keep running and win the race

or

do I go and help my friend?

So, I ran back to check on Samantha and I lost the race. To my amazement, everyone started shouting,

YEAH!!!

QUICK SILVER

YEAH!!!

Samantha couldn't believe that I would come back to help her after she hurt my feelings in the cafeteria. But I told her, "That's what friends do for each other." Samantha apologized to me, and we gave each other a big hug. Although I didn't win first place that day, I did get my #1 friend back and that was winning in my book.

Made in the USA
Charleston, SC
22 June 2016